FROGGY RIDES A BIKE

FROGGY RIDES A BIKE

by JONATHAN LONDON
illustrated by FRANK REMKIEWICZ

PUFFIN BOOKS

For Spencer and Macy, who inspired this story,
and for Sean, Aaron, Natalia, Abby, and Shai—who did, too
      —J.L.

For the children of New Orleans
      —F.R.

PUFFIN BOOKS
Published by the Penguin Group
Penguin Young Readers Group, 345 Hudson Street, New York, New York 10014, U.S.A.
Penguin Group (Canada), 90 Eglinton Avenue East, Suite 700, Toronto, Ontario, Canada M4P 2Y3
(a division of Pearson Penguin Canada Inc.)
Penguin Books Ltd, 80 Strand, London WC2R 0RL, England
Penguin Ireland, 25 St Stephen's Green, Dublin 2, Ireland (a division of Penguin Books Ltd)
Penguin Group (Australia), 250 Camberwell Road, Camberwell, Victoria 3124, Australia
(a division of Pearson Australia Group Pty Ltd)
Penguin Books India Pvt Ltd, 11 Community Centre, Panchsheel Park, New Delhi - 110 017, India
Penguin Group (NZ), 67 Apollo Drive, Rosedale, North Shore 0632, New Zealand
(a division of Pearson New Zealand Ltd)
Penguin Books (South Africa) (Pty) Ltd, 24 Sturdee Avenue, Rosebank, Johannesburg 2196, South Africa

Registered Offices: Penguin Books Ltd, 80 Strand, London WC2R 0RL, England

First published in the United States of America by Viking, a division of Penguin Young Readers Group, 2006
Published by Puffin Books, a division of Penguin Young Readers Group, 2008

25 24 23 22 21 20 19 18 17

Text copyright © Jonathan London, 2006
Illustrations copyright © Frank Remkiewicz, 2006
All rights reserved

THE LIBRARY OF CONGRESS HAS CATALOGED THE VIKING EDITION AS FOLLOWS:
London, Jonathan, date—
Froggy rides a bike / by Jonathan London ; illustrated by Frank Remkiewicz.
p. cm.
Summary: With encouragement from his friends and family, Froggy learns how to ride his shiny new bike.
ISBN: 978-0-670-06099-3 (hc)
[1. Bicycles and bicycling—Fiction. 2. Frogs—Fiction.] I. Remkiewicz, Frank, ill. II. Title.
PZ7.L8432Frq 2006 [E]—dc22 2005018084

Puffin Books ISBN 978-0-14-241067-7

Set in Kabel
Manufactured in China

Froggy looked out the window.
His shiny new bike gleamed in the sun.
"Yippee!" he said . . .

and he flopped outside
and hopped on his bike—*flop flop . . . bing!*—
and took off.

He pedaled so fast
that soon he was going about
a million miles an hour!

He pedaled so fast
that soon he was flying
high in the sky—

WHEEEEE!

And there was his dad
far, far below, calling,

FRROOGGYY!

Froggy stopped flying.

He was falling . . .

falling . . .

He woke up and rubbed his eyes.
"Rise and shine, Froggy!" said his dad.
"Today's the day we get your bike!"

"Yippee!" cried Froggy.
He bounced out of bed and flopped
into the kitchen—*flop flop flop!*

"Let's go," said Froggy.
"Okay," said his dad.
"But first you have to get dressed!"
"Oops!" said Froggy.

And he flopped back
to his bedroom
to get dressed—
*zip! zoop! zup!
zut! zut! zut!*

At the bike shop,
Froggy said, "I want a *trick* bike!"
"But, Froggy," said his dad,
"first you have to learn
how to ride a bike!"

"Okay," said Froggy.
"But I get to pick
it out! That one!"
"Too big," said Dad.

"That one!"
"Too expensive," said Dad.

"*That* one!" said Froggy
"It's the bike of my dreams!"

"Okey-doke!" said Dad.
"Yippee!" cried Froggy.
"My very first bike!
But now I need a horn and a bell!"
"Both?" said Dad. "Okey-doke!"
And Froggy got a horn and a bell—
honk honk! ting-a-ling!

Back at home,
everybody gathered around to watch.
All of Froggy's friends were there—
even Frogilina.
"Okay, Froggy," said his dad.
"Now hop on and pedal like mad.
I won't let go!"

"Okay," said Froggy.
"But first you have to put my horn on. And my bell.
Then I'll ride my bike!"

Froggy's dad put his
horn on—*honk honk!*
"Now hop on and pedal like
mad," he said.
"I won't let go."
"Okay," said Froggy.
"But you still have to
put my bell on.
Then I'll ride my bike!"

Froggy's dad put his bell on—*ting-a-ling!*
"Now hop on and pedal like mad," he said.
"I won't let go."

So Froggy hopped on his bike—*flop flop . . . bing!*—
and pedaled like mad—*honk honk! ting-a-ling!*
zoom zoom zoom!
But then Froggy's dad . . .

"Yikes!" cried Froggy.
His bike zigged and zagged and wobbled.
He was falling . . . falling . . .

Thump! He fell on his bottom.
Frogilina giggled.

Froggy's dad helped him up
and said, "Good job, Froggy!
Now hop on again and pedal like mad!
I won't let go!"

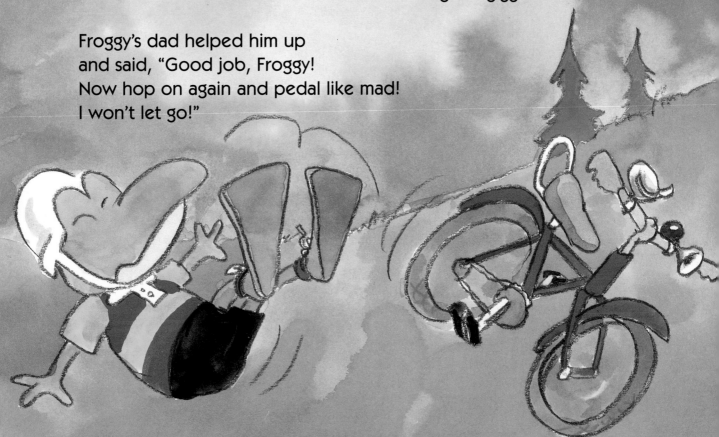

Froggy rubbed his bottom
and hopped on his bike—*flop flop . . . bing!*—
and pedaled like mad—*honk honk! ting-a-ling!*
zoom zoom zoom!
But Froggy's dad . . .
let go again!
Froggy's friends shouted, "Go, Froggy, go!"

"Yikes!" cried Froggy.
His bike zigged and zagged and wobbled.
He was falling . . . falling . . .

But he didn't give up.
He yelled,

WHEEEEE!

and rode his bike . . .

up and down
and up and down
until dinner.

All of Froggy's friends had gone home—
except for Frogilina.
"Watch me!" said Froggy. "No hands!"
And Froggy rode his bike with no hands . . .

right smack into a tree—*thump!*—
and fell on his rump.

"Oops!" cried Froggy,
looking more red in the face than green.
Frogilina laughed.

At dinner, Froggy couldn't sit down.
"What's the matter?" asked his mom.
"My butt's too sore!"
"Fwoggy ga booboo!" giggled Polly.

But in the morning,
Froggy hopped on his bike—*flop flop . . . bing!*
honk honk! ting-a-ling! zoom zoom zoom—
and popped wheelies . . .

all day long—*boing! boing! boing!*